What Anna Loves

Andra Simmons
Illustrated by Gina Capaldi

Heyday Books, Berkeley, California

For Aunt Anna Belle, memories of a special time and place.
For my husband, John, whose artistic vision preserves
a slice of California ranch life. — A. S.

© 2006 by Andra Simmons
Illustrations © 2006 by Gina Capaldi

Heyday Books, founded in 1974, works to deepen people's understanding and appreciation of the cultural, artistic, historic, and natural resources of California and the American West. It operates under a 501(c)(3) nonprofit educational organization (Heyday Institute) and, in addition to publishing books, sponsors a wide range of programs, outreach, and events.

To help support Heyday or to learn more about us, visit our website at www.heydaybooks.com, or write to us at P.O. Box 9145, Berkeley, CA 94709.

Library of Congress Cataloging-in-Publication Data

Simmons, Andra, 1939-
  What Anna loves / Andra Simmons ; illustrated by Gina Capaldi.
      p. cm.
  Summary: Describes life for a young girl on a family-run ranch, as she packs oranges, helps mend fences, mucks out stalls, and enjoys a picnic with her family. Includes facts about the Hurst Ranch in West Covina, California.
    ISBN 1-59714-044-9 (hardcover : alk. paper)
    [1. Ranch life--California--Fiction. 2. California--Fiction. 3. Stories in rhyme.] I. Capaldi, Gina, ill. II. Title.
    PZ8.3.S5864Wh 2006
    [E]--dc22
                                    2006013392

Book design by Lorraine Rath

Printed in China by Phoenix Asia

10 9 8 7 6 5 4 3 2 1

California mornings.
    Lace curtains a-flutter.

Grandma's spice muffins
        all melty with butter.

Buckets that
clatter,

noisy barn chatter.

Grandpa's boots stomping,
farm fields for romping.

Rows ready for seeding,
shady nooks for reading.

A special rope swing,
orange blossoms in spring.

That's what Anna loves.

A hide–and–seek day.
Cool splish-splashy play.

Small walnut-shell boats,
big inner tube floats.

Oranges for packing,
  boxes for stacking.

Grandpa's truck bumping,
Barkley's tail thumping.

Fence mending with Slim,
troughs filled to the brim.

Hay bales to climb, wild giddy-up time.

That's what Anna loves.

Straw hats and bandanas,
hot, dry Santa Anas.

Sycamores for shade,
ice-cold lemonade.

A cowgirl lunch,
crisp cookies to munch.

Is there anything Anna doesn't love?

swarming bees in the air.

Stinging ants everywhere,

Grandma's mean honking goose,

Grandpa's mules
on the loose.

Mucking out smelly stalls,

stinky clothes when she falls.

Raking up rotten fruit,

a mushy mess on her boot.

That's what Anna doesn't love.

Anna loves
    plump berries for picking, big bowls for licking.
    Dessert in the making, fresh cobbler a-baking.

The smell of soft leather.
The family together.

A lazy hayride,
picnicking outside.

Grandpa's grill smoking. Laughing and joking.

A dozy sun sinking…

A velvet sky winking.

Guitar strings a-strumming,
night voices a-humming.

The whisper of Fall,
Old Hooty Owl's call.

That's what Anna loves.

California evenings,
a lemonade moon.

Anna is yawning,
bedtime's coming soon.

So, goodnight to clatter, chatter, and stomping,

humming and strumming, leaping and romping.

Goodnight to the horses, chicks, mules, goats, and geese,

Cozy beds for them all. The barnyard's at peace.

Goodnight to everything Anna loves…

…and even the things she doesn't.

An Author Looks Back...

What Anna Loves is based on the Author's memories of growing up during the 1950s on her family's ranch in West Covina, California. The Hurst Ranch began in 1906 and remained a family business for more than sixty years.

California ranch life in the early 1900s was backbreaking. Today, even with cutting-edge technology and modern machinery, tending the land and raising livestock is still hard work. A typical day on a California ranch often begins at sunrise and ends at sunset—weekends too! For many families, this way of life connects them to the earth and to each other. It is rich in history and traditions, and that's just the way they like it.

Children often helped with the family farm chores, especially during summer vacation. The Hurst children graded onions, mucked out stalls, fed livestock, and drove tractors.

On summer mornings, they slopped through the muddy rows moving crop irrigation sprinklers. Of course, it wasn't all work and no play. In 1924, the Author's grandfather, Charlie Hurst, built a swimming pool on the ranch for all of the children in the community to enjoy. It was icy cold (no heater) and definitely the place to be on a hot summer day.

During her childhood, the Author spent many lazy summer afternoons in that very pool. When she wasn't swimming, Andra could usually be found perched in her favorite walnut tree reading a Nancy Drew mystery or riding to the packinghouse in the old red truck with her dad and dog.

She remembers summer Sundays as special times. The entire family would gather for a swim, a barbecue supper, and a freezer of her dad's homemade ice cream.

In 1998 the Hurst family donated the last remaining three and a half acres of the original 140-acre ranch—including a farmhouse, barns, outbuildings, and artifacts—to become a historical museum. The Hurst Ranch Foundation, in partnership with the City of West Covina, now offers this special place for all to enjoy a slice of California ranch life.

Learn more about this fourth-generation California author, Hurst family history, and ranch life by visiting Andra's website at www.andrasimmons.net.

Sit-down Strike. Beck the mule, circa 1906.

Buggy Ride. The Author's great-grandfather Josiah and dogs, circa 1910.

On Top of the World. The Author's Aunt Anna Belle and Gypsy, circa 1916.

Got Milk? Josiah and Clover, circa 1912.

Saddled Up. The Author's father, Joe, on Sauntee, circa 1916.

A Walk with Grandpa. Josiah, Anna Belle, and Joe, circa 1918.

A Wagon Ride. Anna Belle and Joe, circa 1918.

Bringing in the Harvest. Alfalfa and walnuts, circa 1920.

End of a Long Day. The Author's grandfather Charlie on Sauntee, circa 1920.